XXX STORIES

6 DIRTY STORIES IN 1

I0547862

Erotica Short Stories, Vol. 7

JUST PLAIN BOB

WARNING

This book contains sexually explicit scenes and adult language. It may be considered offensive to some readers. This book is for sale to adults ONLY.

* *

Please store your files wisely where they cannot be accessed by underage readers.

Please feel free to send me an email. Just know that these emails are filtered by my publisher. Good news is always welcome.

Just Plain Bob - **justplainbob@awesomeauthors.org**

About the Publisher

4Fun Publishing, a member of **BLVNP Incorporated**, 340 S. Lemon #6200, Walnut CA 91789, info@blvnp.com / legal@blvnp.com
NOTE: Due to the highly emotional reaction of some people to works of erotic fiction, any email sent to the above address that contains foul language or religious references is automatically deleted by our anti-spam software and will not be seen. All other communications are welcome.

DISCLAIMER
Please don't be stupid and kill yourself. This book is a work of FICTION. Do not try any new sexual practice that you find in this book. It is fiction and not to be confused with reality. Neither the author nor the publisher or its associates assume any responsibility for any loss, injury, death or legal consequences resulting from acting on the contents in this book. Every character in this book is over 18 years of age. The author's opinions are not to be construed as the opinions of the publisher. The material in this book is for entertainment purposes ONLY. Enjoy.

Erotica Short Stories, Vol. 7

XXX Stories

6 Dirty Stories in 1

By: Just Plain Bob

© **Just Plain Bob 2015**
ISBN: 978-1-68030-268-4

Table of Contents

Leslie Visits Family

Older Sluts

Paula, Nick and Eddie

Sally, Brad and Glen

Terry Blindfolded

Vonda's Scoreboard

Leslie Visits Family

I've not had much experience in these matters, actually, no experience at all, but I would guess that most men become highly upset when they find out that their wife is out spreading it around. I know I was. I have no idea how long she has been doing it or what the outcome is going to be when she finally comes home; the only thing I know for sure is that I caught her with her pants down (no pun intended).

Leslie and I have been married for twenty-one years and I suppose our marriage is pretty much the same as that of other middle class couples in the early forties. We were (I almost said are, but I'm not sure about that anymore) comfortable together, had a fairly active sex life and, or least I had thought, both loved and liked each other.

Leslie is a schoolteacher and I am in sales and this has made our marriage somewhat different in that she has a good deal more time off than I do. She has basically the entire summer off, plus spring break, and Christmas vacation. I get three weeks paid vacation a year. Leslie gets eleven paid holidays and I get six so she has a lot of free time that I don't get to share with her. It hasn't been a major problem because of two simple facts: I can't stand her family (neither can she most of the time) and they live four hundred miles away.

Leslie usually takes three weeks off during the summer and goes back to visit them and she always tells them I couldn't come because I don't have enough seniority to bid for summer vacation time. This has been the case for the last ten years now and probably would have been the case for the next ten except for the fickle finger of fate.

It was summer and Leslie had gone back to visit her family. She'd been gone a week when my boss called me in the office and asked me if I would like a company paid mini-vacation. It seems that one of our biggest customers was opening a new branch office about thirty miles from where Leslie was visiting her folks. He wanted me to go and meet the customer, go through the new facility with him and see what we needed to do to get the proper inventory and equipment in place.

"Go over on Thursday and then take Friday off and spend the weekend with Leslie."

I didn't bother to tell him that while spending a weekend with Leslie would be great; a weekend with Leslie and her family would be purgatory. The drive was uneventful and I checked into a motel about half a mile from the new facility and called Leslie to let her know that I was only thirty miles away and would be there for the weekend.

Her sister answered the phone and told me that Leslie wasn't there, that she'd gone shopping. I didn't tell her sister where I was, I just asked her to tell Leslie I had called. Then I went over to the new facility and met Burt, the customer, and we toured the new place together and he outlined what he wanted. I made some suggestions about what he might like to do and then he pointed me to an empty office and I settled in to draft a plan to cover what we had talked about.

We broke for lunch about one o'clock and I made another quick phone call to try and catch Leslie, but she still wasn't back yet. Burt sprang for lunch and when we had finished eating he said:

"Can I ask you something personal?"

I said, "I guess so."

And then he asked me when was the last time I got laid. I told him that it had been over a week ago, just before my wife had gone to visit her family and then I asked him, "Why?"

"I don't know," he said, "You just looked like you needed to get laid. I got a thing laid on for later this afternoon and I just thought I might ask you to join in."

I asked him what kind of a thing and he told me about a woman he'd met in a bar earlier in the week and that she just loved to fuck. She had worn him out and when he hadn't been able to get it up anymore she had asked him if he could call someone to help him put out "her fire". Since then he had seen her every night, always with four or five buddies.

"And she takes us all on and leaves us worn out. I thought maybe you might like to join us tonight."

I have to admit I was tempted, not just because I was horny in anticipation of seeing Leslie, but because I had never taken part in a gangbang and I was curious about what kind of woman would take on a group of guys. I thanked Burt for the invite, but told him I'd be driving over to see my wife who was visiting with family.

"No problem," he said, "But could I ask you a favor? I have to drop my car off at the dealership for some warranty work. Can you drop me at my brother's house? That's where she is meeting us."

I told him I would and then we went back to the new facility and got back to work.

I finished the proposal around five and gave it to Burt for his approval and signature and while he was going over it I tried calling Leslie again. This time I got her brother and he told me that she and her sister had gone out for a bite to eat and he wasn't sure when she'd be back. Burt handed me the signed proposal, we locked the place up and he gave me directions to his brother's house. On the way he tried to talk me into joining him.

"If you don't, you're going to miss the best piece of ass that I've ever seen. Tall, long red hair, and legs that go from the floor all the way up to her ears."

Little did he know, I thought, that I'm on my way to meet one just like that, and I'm not going to have to share." We pulled up in front of his brother's house and my heart stopped, my blood ran cold, and I hit the brakes so hard that Burt's head almost hit the windshield. Burt looked at me:

"What's wrong? You're white as a sheet. You look like you've just seen a ghost."

I mumbled something about a stomach cramp. "It must have been something I ate at lunch and it just hit me."

There, in his brother's driveway, sat the green 1993 Ford Mustang convertible that I had given Leslie for her birthday. There was no chance that it was a car that looked like hers, not with the personalized plate that said LESLIE on the back. Burt suggested that I come in with him and get a glass of water or something, but I told him I would be all right.

"Just go on in and have fun," I told him.

As I drove away my stomach was churning and I felt like I was going to throw up. As soon as I was out of sight of the house I pulled over and parked. There had to be some mistake! Leslie must have loaned her car to her sister or something like that. Maybe her brother was one of Burt's buddies and he was using the car. I started to pull away from the curb and then I stopped - I had to know!

Daylight savings time had just kicked in and even though it was only six o'clock it was already dark and I got out of the car and walked back to the house. I wanted to walk right up to the front door and ring the bell, but I was afraid that I make a fool out of myself in front of Burt and that might jeopardize our business dealings and that wasn't what my boss had sent me down to do.

I started walking around the house looking for a window that would let me see inside. I found several, but they only looked in on empty rooms. I had covered one side and the back of the house when I finally came to a window that let me see into a bedroom. One look and a great weight was lifted from my heart. There were five guys in the room and they were busy stuffing cocks into every hole that Millie, Leslie's sister, had to offer.

My eyes were riveted on the scene taking place in front of me. I would never have thought that Millie would be capable of what she was doing and of looking so sexy while doing it. I also never would have believed that watching her do it would make my dick hard as a rock, but it had, and the evidence was in my hand. I was not even aware that I had taken it out, but there it was and I was stroking it to beat the band and wishing I'd told Burt That I'd join him in fucking that sexy, lust crazed blond.

Blond?

Burt told me he was going to be fucking a redhead. And then I noticed that Burt was not one of the five guys in the room. I moved to the next window; it was another bedroom and what was taking place in it caused my hard cock to wilt like a piece of overcooked noodle. On her hands and knees with a hard cock pounding into her from behind while her mouth moved up and down on the cock of the man lying underneath her, was my wife Leslie.

Standing beside the bed and stroking their cocks while waiting their turn were Burt and two other men. I threw up on the side of the house. I don't even remember walking back to my car or even driving back to the motel. I didn't sleep much that night; constant dreams of Leslie being fucked by hordes of cocks kept moving through my head. In the morning I checked out and drove home.

The phone rang and when I answered it Leslie said, "Good morning, lover. God, but I miss you."

I was silent for a moment and then I said, "When did you find the time to miss me? Before you fucked Burt, his brother, and all of his buddies, or after? Before you met him at the bar for the first time or in between meetings with him and his friends? For that matter, are you just finishing up with them or just getting ready to go meet them again?"

There was silence on the other end, and then a sob, "Oh, baby, I'm so sor...."

But I'd already hung up.

End of the 1st Story

-
-
-
-
-
-
-

Older Sluts

-
-
-
-
-
-

It was the night of my father's funeral and there had been a wake at the house following the burial. It had lasted well into the night and once everyone had gone home I found myself sitting in the kitchen drinking and talking with my mom.

Mostly we reminisced about dad. Mom wasn't all that weepy eyed and truth be told she was relieved that he was gone. That sounds cold, but it really wasn't. He had been sick for such a long time and she had been forced to watch him slowly waste away. She was relieved that his suffering was over and she was relieved that the rest of the family could now move on with their lives.

She was in the middle of describing something that she and dad had done when in their twenties when suddenly she stopped.

"Rob, honey, may I ask you a very personal question?"

I chuckled and said, "You've been doing it for thirty-five years. Why ask now?"

"This is really, really personal, honey."

"Okay, but I reserve the right not to answer."

"Why haven't you married? You are a great looking guy and I've seen the way women look at you, but even though you always seem to have a new girlfriend I've never seen you really serious about one."

Well, there are some things you can never tell your mother no matter how close you are and so I did what I had to – I lied.

"I've just never found the right woman, mom."

The truth of the matter was that I had found the right woman, several of them in fact, but it was a Catch 22. I looked for a specific type of woman and I found plenty of them, but once I found them they were the kind of woman that I could never marry. For one thing they were already married and if by chance I would have found one who was single and who might have turned into the kind of woman I looked for I would have run screaming from her.

I couldn't tell my mother that or even if I could, I could have never explained it satisfactorily to her. And the one thing I could never, ever tell her is that it was her fault. I could just imagine her face if I were to say:

"It is all your fault, mom. If you hadn't run with such a bunch of whorish sluts I wouldn't be the way I am and I would probably be married and you would have grandkids."

No, I couldn't tell her that so I settled for, "I've just never found the right woman."

"Well, Rob, you are still young and there is still time. You will find the right one eventually," and she got up, kissed my cheek and went off to bed. I finished my drink and then I headed on home to my apartment.

<<O>>

I was in my bed staring up at the ceiling and for some weird reason my mind went to work on what it would have gone like if I had given mom an honest answer to her question.

"The reason I'm not married mom is because most of your girlfriends were round heeled tramps."

"And just how did that keep you from getting married?"

"Do you remember that Fraternal Order of Eagles dance that you talked me into going to on my nineteenth birthday?"

"Vaguely."

"Dad was out of town on business. There was Beth, her husband Mark, Dorothy and her husband Don, and you and me. Back then the legal age for drinking was eighteen and Dorothy and Beth though that it would be a kick to get me loaded on my birthday and they kept buying me mixed drinks. What they didn't know was that I didn't like hard liquor and that I was pouring the booze out and not drinking it. They drank theirs though and after a while they had a good buzz on.

"Somewhere along the way they got the idea that it would be fun to cock tease the birthday boy. They started taking turns dragging me out onto the dance floor and every time they had their backs to their husbands they would press their bodies into mine. I was young, the hormones were raging and two sexy older women rubbing themselves against me got me erect in a hurry and then it got worse. Once they felt the erection they constantly rubbed against it and whispered things like:

"Is that a roll of quarters in your pocket or are you just glad to be with me."

"Dorothy even asked me if I would go outside with her for some fresh air and take my dick out and show it to her."

"I hardly see where any of that would have kept you from getting married.

"Be patient, I'll get to it. Anyway, by the time we left the dance I had a huge case of blue balls. When it came time to get in the car Mark was driving and you and Don got up front with him and I ended up in the back sitting between Dorothy and Beth. We weren't even out of the parking lot before Beth put her hand on the bulge in my pants and started rubbing it. As soon as she was sure it was hard she started talking to you and her husband about the band and how good it had been and how their song selection had included so many of her favorites. While she was talking she unzipped my pants, took my cock out and started giving me a hand job.

At the same time Dorothy took my hand and took it up under her dress and put it on her pussy. She leaned over, nibbled on my ear lobe and whispered:

"Finger fuck me, honey. Get me off while Beth gets you off."

"So there we were roaring down the highway with both women carrying on conversations with you and their husbands while playing around with me. The entire time I sat there scared to death that Mark, Don or you would turn around and see what was going on, but none of you ever did. Beth just kept talking to Mark and beating me off and soon I could feel myself getting ready to cum. Beth must have sensed it and she lowered her head and took me in her mouth. As soon as her lips clamped around my rod I blew.

"While Beth's mouth was busy on me Dorothy kept up the conversation with you guys up front. Beth finished draining me dry and as soon as she pulled her head away from me I went to stuff my cock back into my pants, but Dorothy pushed my hand away and took my limp cock in her hand. She worked at getting me hard again while she and Beth kept up conversations with you, Mark and Don.

"It was exciting as hell to have two married women, both old enough to be my mother, playing with my cock while having casual conversations with their significant others. Dorothy was a little bolder than Beth and as soon as my cock started stirring she bent down and started giving me a blow job. Beth sat there and watched as she chatted away with the three of you up front. About two blocks from our house Dot managed to get me to blast a load down her throat and I was just zipping up as we pulled into our driveway. It was one hell of a birthday, one that I damned sure will never forget."

"And that kept you from getting married?"

"That was the start of it. There is more, but first I have a question for you. Those were the girls you ran with and I've always wondered about that. The old 'birds of a feather flock together' thing."

She blushed and looked away as she said, "Honestly, Rob, how can you ask your mother a thing like that," and I had my answer. I wondered if my dad knew or suspected. She moved quickly to get me away from questions about her:

"I still don't see how Dot and Beth kept you from getting married."

"The day after the night at the Eagles, Dot called me and told me that Don was out of town for two days and she needed some help to move some things and could I come over and help her. I jumped at the chance and why not? She had sucked my cock in a car full of people and with her husband not three feet away so God only knew what she might do if we were alone. She told me to be there at seven-thirty that evening and I told her I was looking forward to helping her. She giggled and said:

"I'll just bet you are, you naughty boy you. And honey? Don't let your mom know okay? It will just make her nervous."

I got there at seven-twenty and when she answered the door she was wearing a pair of high heels and not a stitch of anything else. I was stunned. She was my first fully naked woman and my heart nearly stopped. I'd seen naked women in Playboy, Penthouse and other magazines, but Dorothy was real and she was just standing there and all I had to do was reach out a hand and I could touch her. She saw my expression and an amused smile appeared on her face.

"You are a little early, honey; a tad eager, are we?"

I probably blushed and she laughed. "That's okay, honey, I like that in a man," and she ran a hand down my front to my already iron bar like cock and giggled, "Yep, eager. Come on, honey, let's not waste it," and she took me by the hand and led me to her bedroom.

It is what I was hoping would happen, but I was a little unnerved by the 'cut and dried' aspect of it. So much so that I mumbled something inane:

"Weren't we going to move some furniture or something?" and Dorothy, or Dot as she asked me to call her, laughed and said, "If we do it right, honey, the bed will move all over the place. If you want to move something, move that phone over to where I can reach it from the bed."

I thought that curious, but I moved it and then Dot pushed me back on the bed and began pulling my pants off me. As soon as my cock was exposed she took it in her mouth and started giving me a blow job. After a minute or so she stopped long enough to tell me to take my shirt off and after I had she went back to sucking my cock. Her hands fondled my balls and one finger teased my asshole as her hot mouth was driving me crazy. I started bucking my hips up at her face and I could feel myself close to cumming. She had her hands on my balls and she must have felt something for I felt her lips clamp tight around my cock and she shoved her finger in my ass. I arched up off the bed and came so hard I was surprised that I didn't see cum squirt out her ears. She sucked every drop out of me and then she pulled her mouth off me and said:

"I always like to get the first one out of the way quickly; it makes the next couple last a lot longer. What can we do while we wait for you to get hard again? Do you eat pussy, honey?"

The look on my face gave her the answer to that one and she said, "No matter, honey, you will before I'm done with you. For now why don't you suck my tits and finger fuck me while my hands work on you."

She proceeded to show me how she liked her tits handled, what spot in her pussy I should rub to give her the most pleasure and the entire time I did that she was using her hands on me and talking:

"Yes," she hissed. "Bite the nipple, baby, no need to be gentle with me; I'm a slut and you can treat me like one. I'm going to fuck your eyes out, honey; I'm going to turn you into my fuck toy. Think you can stand it, honey? Think you are up to being my very own personal fuck toy?"

My cock twitched and she giggled and said, "He seems to like the idea."

She slid down and took me in her mouth and started sucking me until I was hard. When it was stiff enough to suit her she swung herself over me and used a hand to guide me into her as she sat down on my dick. She leaned forward as she started to ride me and her tits dangled in my face.

"Lick my nipples, honey, suck my tits," and when I did what she had asked she moaned and slammed her cunt down on me. She had already gotten me off once so I lasted for a while as she rode me and told me how she planned on fucking me to death.

"I'm going to jack you off, honey, suck your cock and fuck you with my ass and pussy. I'm going to turn you into my love slave, honey. I'm going to make sure that you never want to be more than a mile away from my pussy. Does that turn you on, honey? Does it excite you to know that I'm going to make you my fuck toy?"

She was lying next to me, fondling my cock and balls and trying to get me up for another romp and she was making some progress. My cock was twitching in her hand as it struggled to get upright again. The phone rang and Dot looked at her watch.

"Right on time," she said and she gave my cock a little squeeze. "Hurry, baby, I need you hard for this."

She reached for the phone and answered it:

"Hello? Oh hi, baby, miss me?"

With one hand holding the phone to her ear and the other playing with my cock she said, "Just lying here in bed and thinking of you. Same as always, baby. Thinking of your hard cock and what we could be doing with it if you were here."

My cock was shooting up and Dot started stroking it.

"I can almost feel it in my hand, baby. It was soft and pliable when I first touched it, but now it is growing into a hard steel bar. Yes, baby, oh yes. Are you where you can take your cock out? Do it. Okay, baby, feel my hand on it? Feel my fingers flutter over your cockhead? Feel them wrap around you and slowly start to stroke?"

She shifted position on the bed until her mouth was only inches away from my dick.

"I can see the veins start to pulse, baby, I feel you throb in my hand. I lower my head and stick my tongue out and lick it," and as she said that, she did it to me.

"I want to suck on it, baby, but you tell me no. You say you are hot and ready to fuck me and you don't want to waste time on a blow job. You make me get in your favorite position," and with that she got on her hands and knees.

"You push a finger into my steaming pussy," and she motioned for me to do that. As I slid a finger into her sopping wet pussy, I caught on to what was happening. I may have been only nineteen and a little naïve, but I understood that I was supposed to do what she described to her husband as she described it.

"You work the finger around and I moan and ask you to hurry up and fuck me, but you don't. You put another finger in me and then another and finger fuck me."

I did what she said and she moaned again.

"God, baby, you have me so hot I'm going to set the bed sheets on fire if you don't use your hose to cool me down. Please, baby, please fuck me. I cry and you pull out your fingers and move behind me. You poke your hard cock at my pussy and I cry out as you slam your iron hard cock into me."

I pushed hard and slid into her and she cried out, "Oh God, baby, it feels so fucking good. Fuck me, lover, fuck me hard. Make me cum, baby, make me cum."

I pounded my cock into her hot steaming cunt and bit my lip to keep from making noises that Don might hear. Dot pushed back at me on each of my in strokes as she kept up her telephone sex with Don.

"Hard, baby, push it deep. I want to feel it all the way up to my throat, baby, drive it deep."

I was fucking her as hard as I could and sweat was dripping off me. I wanted to shoot my load deep in her and I was trying hard to cum while she still had Don on the phone, but the dog position didn't seem to give me what I needed. I pulled out of Dot and pushed her over on her back. She spread her legs wide and grinned up at me. I grabbed her legs and put them up on my shoulders and then I drove my cock into her.

"Oh Jesus God, baby, it feels so good. Push that hard cock into me, push it deep and fuck me hard. Make me cum, baby, make me cum."

I felt her cunt muscles try to grip me and I rammed her hard.

"Oh God yes, baby, yes baby, yes. Harder, baby, harder, fuck me harder. Oh god, oh god, I'm cumming, I'm cumming, oh sweet fucking Jesus yes, yes yes yes," she screamed and her whole body trembled as she had her orgasm.

Her cunt felt like it was trying to suck me in and I blew my load and collapsed on the bed next to her. She threw a leg over me and her hand found my deflated dick and she fondled it as she said:

"That was good, baby, that was good. Of course I came, didn't you hear me scream? No, baby, I didn't use my fingers because they aren't long enough or hard enough. I had to use something long and hard," and she gave my cock a squeeze.

"I used my hair brush. Maybe you need to find one of those adult stores and buy me a nice fat, long and hard dildo. If we do this too often I'm afraid my hair brush won't survive. Love you too, baby. Talk to you later."

She tossed the phone on the pillow and slid down the bed so her mouth was inches from my cock and she looked up at me and grinned.

"How about it, honey? Think you might like to be my fuck toy?" and then her mouth latched onto my cock and she went to work at getting me up again.

<<O>>

The next day I had just gotten home from class when the phone rang. I answered it and it was Beth.

"I hear that you went over to that bitch's house last night. I was supposed to be the first one to get you."

"You were supposed to be first? What did you do, flip a coin? She called and asked me to come over and help her move some things and I did."

"The whore knew I was going to call you and she just couldn't stand the idea that I might have you first."

"I thought she was your friend?"

"She is, but she is still a whore. Are you doing anything right now?"

"No, I just got home from class."

"Can you come over?"

"Right now?"

"As soon as possible."

I said I would be right over and I put a note on the table telling you that I wouldn't be home for dinner that night and then I left to go visit Beth. When she answered the door to let me in I was surprised to see Mark sitting in the living room watching television. I walked in and looked at her with a question written on my face and she grinned at me.

"Mark, honey, Rob is here to help me move that stuff in the basement. If you need me for anything just holler," and then she took me by the hand and led me down into the basement.

"Mark has a bad back and he has to be careful not to throw it out so he can't help me with the heavy stuff."

She led me over to the corner where the washer and dryer sat and then she raised her skirt and pushed her thong down her legs and kicked it way.

"Help me up on the dryer, sweetie."

I did and she scooted forward until her pussy was right on the edge. I'd have to stand on my tip toes for a straight shot at it, but it could be done. I cast a worried glance up at the ceiling and Beth giggled and said:

"He was a lot closer in the car and we carried it off. Put it in me, sweetie, don't make me wait."

I unzipped and dropped my trousers and boxers, lined myself up with her slit and after one last look toward the ceiling I drove my cock into her.

<<O>>

"And that's the story mom. For the next six years Dorothy and Beth used me as their fuck toy and I gloried in it. I was especially turned on when I fucked them when they were on the phone with their husbands or if the husbands were in the next room or some other place close by. I'd still be their fuck toy if Don hadn't gotten promoted and had to transfer out of the state and Beth hadn't died in that auto accident."

"That doesn't make sense, Rob. So you had an affair, so what? It ended when Dorothy and Don moved to Dayton. How would that keep you from finding a nice girl and getting married?"

"Because after Dorothy and Beth, a nice girl just wouldn't cut it for me. I need sluts, not nice girls. I need to be with married women who cheat on their husbands. I look for married women with husbands who travel. I want to be in his bed fucking his wife when she is on the phone talking to him. I want her legs wrapped tight around me while she is telling him that she loves him and is missing him.

"That, mother dear, is the kind of woman I want and need, but the opposite side of the coin is that I couldn't stand being married to a woman like that. I couldn't leave the house knowing that like as not she would be fucking someone else someday.

"No, mom, your little boy Rob will never be getting married."

The End

-
-
-
-
-
-
-

Paula, Nick and Eddie

-
-
-
-
-
-

Paula and I have been married for fifteen years now and it's been a good marriage. We have two great kids and we have a great family life. We are active in the community and the church and are fairly well known in our town. Paula is a beautiful woman who looks more like a twenty-year-old model than the thirty-six year old housewife that she is. She turns male heads wherever she goes and I long ago got used to it. For the last ten years our sex life has been good, if somewhat routine and predictable and I had no reason to think that it would ever change. Until a Friday night one month ago.

Paula and I had been invited to a party being held by some friends of ours. We were glad to get out of the house and since we knew, and more importantly, liked most of the people who would be there, we were looking forward to it. Paula looked absolutely stunning in a simple white cocktail dress that showed off her great tan and sexy legs and I would have to say that she was by far the best looking woman there that night.

The party was in full swing when we arrived and everyone was having a great time. Somewhere along the way I lost track of Paula. I didn't think much about it because we both like to circulate at these events and talk to the people that we know. Over an hour went by before I saw her again. She was on her way to the ladies room and for some reason I had the thought that she looked somewhat mussed up, but then someone said something to me and I went back to my circulating.

When we got home that night Paula dragged me into the bedroom and was more sexually aggressive than I'd seen her in years. I couldn't believe how wet she was when I entered her or her sexual frenzy as she begged me to fuck her harder and deeper. She had multiple orgasms that night for the first time in years, and as soon as I'd cum she had her mouth on my dick trying to get me hard again. I managed to get it up and off three times before my cock refused to respond again. In frustration, when her mouth couldn't get me up again, she swung over me and ground her pussy down on my face and held it there until I got her off again with my tongue. We both fell into an exhausted sleep.

<<O>>

The next afternoon, following a round of golf, I was sitting on the crapper in one of the stalls in the locker room when a couple of guys came in and began talking about the Friday night party.

"Did you hear about Paula?" said one guy.

"No," said the other.

"From what I hear, Nick and Eddie took her out to Eddie's van and she damn near fucked them to death."

The other guy said, "You're shitting me! Mrs. Perfect?"

"Hey, that's what I hear. My first thought was 'bullshit', but Tom Murray said he saw the three of them get into Eddie's van. So this morning when Nick says she's got a mouth like a vacuum cleaner, I got to hope it's true. I'd love to get a taste of Paula and if she put out for Nick and Eddie maybe there is hope for me."

"Yeah. I know what you mean. Maybe I should go buy a van so I can be ready, just in case."

Locker doors slammed closed and they walked out.

I was not ready for that. In fact there were two things I wasn't ready for - the thought of Paula taking on two of my friends in the back of a van, and the raging hardon that I got hearing about it. Paula had never given me a reason to be jealous and at first I tended to believe that what I'd just heard was someone's wishful thinking. I did not doubt that every man who knew her, or even saw her, would want to fuck her, but she wouldn't, would she? No, I said to myself, she wouldn't, but then I remembered not seeing her for quite a while and then when I did see her she looked a bit mussed. And then there was her aggressive sexual behavior last night. What was behind that? Could she have fucked Nick and Eddie? I was no longer certain that she didn't.

Suspicion is a terrible thing to carry around. I spent days wondering what, if anything, my lovely wife might have done that night. I suppose I could have asked her and I believe that if I had she would have told me truthfully that she had or hadn't, but I also suppose I didn't really want to know for sure. What was really disquieting was that every time I imagined Paula in the back of the van with Nick and Eddie my dick would get rock hard.

Since the night of the party Paula could not get enough sex. She was on me as soon as we got the kids to bed and she did not stop until I was exhausted. A month went by and there never was a day or even an hour that I didn't think about Paula, Nick, Eddie and that goddamn fucking van. Things were not helped any by the snatches of conversation that I would overhear or the rumors that came to my attention. It could have been my imagination, but it seemed to me that everybody was talking about Paula and her sexual escapades. Or was it what everybody was saying about the party being blown all out of proportion? God, but it was eating me up. Finally, one afternoon I just snapped. I got up from my desk at one in the afternoon and headed home. I would ask Paula and put an end to this once and for all.

The first indication that the stories might be true came when I turned onto my street and saw a van that looked a lot like Eddie's parked in front of my house. Was it Eddie's or just one that looked like his that maybe belonged to one of Paula's friends? I decided to park at the end of the block and wait a bit. Twenty minutes later I got my answer. Nick, Eddie and another man I didn't recognize came out of the house, got in the van and drove away. I watched them turn the corner and then I took a deep breath and went on home.

Once in the house I went straight to the bedroom. Paula lay spread out on the bed, legs open, pussy matted with cum and staring at the ceiling. She saw movement out of the corner of her eye and must have thought they had come back. "You want more?" she said, "I thought I did a pretty good job of wearing you out."

"Not hardly," I said.

Paula's head jerked up, she saw me, and with a voice that had so much anguish in it that it almost broke my heart to hear it said, "Oh dear God". Her head fell back to the pillow and she started crying. I was torn. On the one hand I wanted to take her in my arms and comfort her and on the other I wanted to demand an explanation. But there was a third hand. Lying on that bed, freshly fucked, she looked sexier than I'd seen her look in years. In the end however, I turned around and walked back downstairs.

It was half an hour before she came down the stairs. I was in the den watching TV when she came in and sat down on the couch. I turned to look at her, but did not say a word. She started weeping again and after a minute or so it all came tumbling out of her. She'd had several drinks and was in a pretty good mood and had gone outside with Nick and Eddie to catch some fresh air and the next thing she knew she was in the van with them and they were making out. Then they drove to the local lover's lane where they had engaged in no holds barred sex for the next hour. They had done it all - anal, oral, two on one, everything! I shook my head in disbelief. My Paula - loving mother, housewife, volunteer church worker - participating in an orgy! I asked her if she had been taken by force and she said they had taken her by surprise in getting her into the van, but once inside she had enthusiastically cooperated. She said she'd had at least five orgasms and they probably would have stayed longer but a car that thought might be police had scared them away. She said she'd had fantasies for years about making it with other men, but said she had never intended to actually make her fantasies come true. It just happened.

"How about since then?" I asked. "What about today? Are all the rumors that I've been hearing about your sexual escapades true?"

She said she didn't know what I'd heard, but that night with Nick and Eddie she'd found out how great sex could be with multiple partners and they had been getting together two or three times a week ever since.

"Who was that stranger here with them today?"

Paula shrugged, "Just a friend of Eddie's, I think his name was Dave."

"So it hasn't been just Nick and Eddie?" I asked.

"Usually just them, but sometimes they bring a friend or two."

A friend or two, I thought, Christ, now we are talking gangbangs. I just sat there shaking my head. Finally Paula said, "Damn it - say something, don't just sit there staring at me."

I lost it! "What the fuck do you want me to say? Congratulations on becoming the town slut? Kudos for having your name become a household word with everyone we know? Have you got any fucking idea how many people in this town are talking about you and your damn sexual goings on? Do you think I'm home today by accident? I'm here because all I've heard for the last month is how big a fucking whore you are and I had to find out for myself if it was true."

Every sentence caused her to wince as if I was hitting her and I wasn't through yet. "You still want me to say something? Okay! How's this? I'm fucking pissed! I'm pissed that you let it happen. I'm pissed that you didn't trust me enough to tell me what happened that night. I'm pissed that you have been fucking around on me. I'm pissed that for the last month you have been a punch board for men who I thought were my friends and for men I don't even know. But most of all I am pissed because you denied me a chance to be a part of it. You are not the only one who has fantasies. I've got plenty! While watching you fuck other men or fucking you after other men get through using you hasn't been one of them, at least not then, I could have still shared mine with you had you seen fit to share yours with me."

She was still reacting as if every word I said was a blow from a fist, but I was wound up tight and not ready to quit. "I heard about your little escapade the very next day out at the club. I didn't believe it at first - I didn't want to believe it, but even so the image of you in that fucking van with those two guys has been in my head ever since. I have thought about it every day for the last month and every time I think about it my dick gets hard."

She looked at me, "So what do we do now?"

"Why the hell are you asking me? You're the one with the cunt that has to be scratched by groups of guys. I'm just the poor dumb bastard that loves you." She stared at the floor and did not say a word.

"Are you willing to stop fucking other guys?" I asked.

Still staring at the floor she said in a low voice, "If you want me to."

"In other words," I said, "You still want to?"

She looked up at me and said, "Yes. I still want to."

I stared at her for a moment before saying, "Then you have answered your own question, haven't you?" She looked at me questioningly. "About what we are going to do!" I looked at my watch. "For now," I said, "We do nothing. The kids will be home from school in half an hour and you need to wash all that cum off of you before they get here."

I picked up the phone and called the local Motel 6 and made a reservation for eight that night. I looked at Paula and said, "The next move is yours. You can call Nick, Eddie, or whoever you want and however many you want, but understand this - our marriage survives only if I get to be at all of your little get togethers, or at least know about them ahead of time and you tell me about them afterwards. You decide. Meanwhile, I'm going upstairs and get naked. I hear from a reliable source that you have a mouth like a vacuum cleaner and I want to find out if it's true."

Paula stared at me for a moment and then she smiled and reached for the phone.

The End

-
-
-
-
-
-
-

Sally, Brad and Glen

-
-
-
-
-
-
-

Sally and I have been married for a little over twenty-eight years now. Our sexual relationship was great when it started and it has gotten steadily better over the years. Outside of some gray strands showing in her red hair, Sally is still as much of a sexpot as she was when I married her. Five-foot, one hundred and five pounds and a 34-22-32 figure kept nice and tight by regular trips to the gym. Sally has been hit on by guys since the day I met her and she was fairly promiscuous right up to the day we wed, but she has been a loving and faithful wife since that day. So I was somewhat surprised when we got home from a party one night to find that my wife had just been fucked by another man. We had just gotten home and I was horny as hell and wanted to make love. Sally tried to put me off, but I was insistent and as soon as my fingers touched her pussy I knew that all that wetness couldn't have come from just Sally. I pulled back from her and looked at her face and she began to cry.

The party had been a pool party at the home of our friends Marsha and Glen. There were about twelve people there including Glen's cousin Brad who was visiting from out of town. Sally was wearing a little yellow bikini and, as usual, she was producing hard ons all over the place. Most of Glen and Marsha's parties turn into drunkathons so Sally and I take turns being the designated driver and this time was my turn so Sally was really hitting the Margaritas and was feeling no pain. It started to get chilly in the afternoon so Sally went into the house to change out of her bikini and into her regular street clothes. She went into the bathroom, locked the door, and had taken off her bathing suit when the door opened and Brad came in. He stepped inside, locked the door behind him and then smiled and held up the little rod that he had used to trip the bathroom door lock.

"You have teased me all day with that body and I think it is only fair that you should see what you have caused," and he unzipped and took out a hard cock that was every bit of ten inches long.

Sally had grabbed a towel and covered herself when Brad had first walked into the room and when he began to walk toward her, she backed up until her back was against the wall, but even as she backed up she couldn't take her eyes off his huge cock. As he walked toward her he said, "You caused it so you get to take care of it" and he reached out and pulled the towel away from her. He took her right hand and put it on his cock, "You did that, you and your little bikini and it's very uncomfortable walking around with something this large stuck in my trousers so you have to make it go away." He put his hands on her shoulders and turned her and bent her over the sink. Sally knew what he intended to do and she knew she should be fighting to get away from him, but she'd had a lot to drink and she was fascinated by his huge cock and she wondered, after twenty years of just mine, what another cock would feel like, especially one so big.

Besides, she thought, no one would ever know.

Brad pushed her down and Sally bent at the waist and gripped the sides of the sink and waited for Brad to take her. Brad fucked her for almost ten minutes before he came and Sally had orgasms so intense that she had to grab a wash cloth and put it in her mouth to keep everybody in the neighborhood from hearing her screams of pleasure. After he gushed into her he wanted her to suck his cock and get him hard again, but she said no, that she had been gone for too long and she needed to get back to the party before I missed her and came looking for her. Later on during the party Brad approached her again about getting together again during his visit, but by then Sally was on a guilt trip over cheating on me and she wouldn't talk to him.

I was surprised that my wife could have done that to me, but I was even more surprised at how hot and horny her story had made me. I told Sally to stop crying and get her clothes off. "I want sloppy seconds." I fucked the little bitch as hard or harder than I ever had before and I fucked her five times before I couldn't get my dick up anymore. We fell asleep in each other's arms and when I woke up the next morning I did something that I had never done before - I went down on Sally while she still had cum in her. I don't know whose taste was prevalent - mine or Brad's - but I'm guessing that it was mine since I was the last one there and before I was done cleaning out the unfaithful little slut I knew that I just had to taste what Brad tasted like. I fucked Sally until two that afternoon and then we showered and when we were done I wanted to fuck Sally again, but I just could not get my cock hard again.

At two forty-five I told Sally to call Brad and make a date to see him. She looked at me like I was crazy and I told her that the image of her bent over that sink while Brad fucked her from behind was driving me crazy and I wanted her to fuck him again. I told her to call him and tell him I was going out to play golf at four and she'd like it if he could drop by the house.

"Tell him I'll be gone for at least four hours and that you'll have all the time you need to enjoy that huge cock again."

She was reluctant to call him and she told me that it was bad enough that she had cheated on me the one time and that she couldn't do it again. I explained to her that it wouldn't be cheating on me if I knew about it and wanted her to do it.

"For Christ's sake, Sally, look at what I've been doing since we got home last night. I'm as turned on by this as you were when he first slid that huge cock into your tight little pussy."

In the end she called Brad and I sat next to her on the couch and listened to her tell Brad how much she had enjoyed being stuffed by him and she wanted to do it again.

I was in the closet when Brad arrived and I watched through the partially open door as Brad turned Sally every which way but loose on our bed. I was truly amazed to see that huge thing going into my little Sally and I was even more amazed at the wanton slut she became as he fucked her time after time. She was begging him to fuck her harder and to never stop and between bouts she told him that she was his slut to do with what he wanted for as long as he was in town.

I went from amazed to astounded when she asked Brad to take her in her ass. We only occasionally engage in anal sex because even my average six and a half inches hurts Sally too much. She loves ass fucking, but can only handle about four or five minutes of it before she starts to hurt too badly. She got the KY out of the bedside stand and Brad worked on her ass with thumb and fingers for a good five minutes before he positioned himself behind her and began to push home. Sally bit down on a mouthful of pillow to keep from screaming as Brad moved more and more of his stiff pole into her and then he began long, slow strokes and Sally began to moan. Brad fucked her slowly for about two minutes and then Sally screamed and had an orgasm and then bit into the pillow again and waited for him to cum. She had asked him to fuck her in the ass and she was going to fight the discomfort until he came. Brad must have been used to ass fucking his women with that big dick and he apparently knew when it was becoming uncomfortable for them and so he pulled out of Sally and walked into the bathroom and washed his cock. Then he came back and rolled her onto her back and fucked her again.

At seven Sally told him he needed to leave just in case I came home a little early and Brad asked her if he could see her again. Sally threw a quick glance at the closet and then she told him that she had already told him that she was his slut for as long as he was in town.

"Tomorrow then?" he asked.

"My husband leaves for work at seven and doesn't get home until five-thirty. Will that give you enough time?"

He grinned at her. "I'll be parked on the corner watching for him to leave."

When he was gone I came out of the closet and went after her like a sex maniac. I slurped all of Brad out of her that I could and then I fucked her until I couldn't get hard anymore. I finally fell asleep, totally exhausted, around two in the morning.

Brad was in town for ten days and on every one of those ten days he fucked Sally. Sometimes I was able to be home and watch from the closet, but most of the time I had to be at work, but either way the first thing I did when Brad left or when I got home from work was to eat Sally's pussy and then fuck her. I have no idea why I got so much enjoyment out of eating her after another man had finished fucking her, but I got to the point where I craved it. I was already thinking about how I was going find someone else to fuck Sally when Brad was gone and I didn't think that Sally was going to complain much. The more Brad fucked her, the more I fucked her and Sally was loving it. The two of us, Sally and I, had more sex in that ten-day period than we'd had in the previous three months.

Then on the tenth day Brad took care of my problem for me. Since it was his last day in town I had taken the day off work so I could watch his farewell performance. He had fucked Sally for almost two hours and then he said, "I know that this isn't love, just sex, but it is obvious to me that you love my size and I feel guilty about getting you started on my big cock and then taking it away from you so I have arranged for a replacement until I can come and visit again. Come on in, cousin," and Glen walked into the bedroom. His cock was every bit as long as Brad's, but his was a little fatter. Sally really wasn't interested in getting a reputation as a slut and she protested, but Brad was on top of her and working his cock in and out of her pussy and she couldn't get up and run away. Brad was fucking her hard and Glen kept trying to poke his cock into her mouth, but Sally kept turning her head away to avoid it. Then she had a huge orgasm and when her mouth opened up to scream Glen had pushed his cock into it. By the time Brad had cum Sally was avidly sucking on Glen's cock and was disappointed when Glen took it away from her so that he could take Brad's place between her legs. The two of them took turns fucking her for the rest of the afternoon. When they left and I came charging out of the closet, I could barely feel her when I fucked her, but it didn't matter - I got off just soaking in her hot, cum filled cunt.

Glen has been fucking Sally for almost five months now. They get together on the average of three times a week, but apparently what Glen is giving her and what she gets from me is not enough to satisfy her newfound cock hunger. She loved the threesome she had with Glen and Brad and she wants to have some more of them. Last night I gave Sally a surprise. She had spent the afternoon with Glen and was waiting for me when I got home with her legs spread wide and her pussy dripping. I buried my face in her snatch and licked and sucked her clean and then I said, "I don't think you're hot enough for me to fuck yet," and I got up off the bed and my best friend walked into the room. "Dale can fuck you a couple of times and then when you are good and hot I'll join in."

Dale didn't leave until three in the morning, but by the time he left we had fucked Sally so much that she asked us to give her a rest. Dale and I did things to Sally that I had never even heard of before. We had both fucked her at the same time three different times; once Dale was in her ass and I was in her pussy, once I was in her ass and Dale was in her pussy and the third time we were both in her pussy - at the same time! Sally had screamed in pleasure and later, when she had asked us to give her a rest I said, "Okay. Same time tomorrow?" She nodded her head yes, her head hit the pillow and she was out for the night.

This morning, just before I left for work, the phone rang and Sally answered it. It was from Brad and he was in town for two weeks and he wanted to know if Sally would like to see him. She told him to hang on for a second, that her water for coffee was boiling over. She covered the mouthpiece with her hand, told me who it was and what he wanted. "Don't ask me," I said, "You've got me, Dale and Glen all trying to wear out your cunt. Can you handle all of us and Brad too?"

Sally looked at me and smiled and then put the phone back up to her ear. "Brad, honey, as many times as we can in the time you are here." She hung up the phone, "Hurry off to work, baby. He's on the way over and we wouldn't want the two of you meeting at the front door, now would we?"

The End

Terry Blindfolded

I probably never would have found out if she hadn't come home drunk that night. In high school and in college I'd taken part in several gangbangs and you never forget what it feels like to slip your cock in a cum filled hole. I'd undressed her and had looked down on her lying on the bed with her legs spread, giggling at something only she could see and she looked so damn sexy that I just had to fuck her. My cock slid right in and I knew immediately that I wasn't the first one to fuck her that night, or even the second or third. I thought back to the gangbangs I'd been a part of and I tried to imagine Terry lying on her back with a line of guys waiting for their turn and the image drove me crazy. I fucked her three times before I rolled over and went to sleep.

Terry and I had been married almost three years and early on in our relationship we had reached an accommodation on personal space. We both realized we needed to spend a little time away from each other and that we each needed an outside activity or two. For me it was bowling on Thursday night and golf on either Saturday or Sunday mornings. For Terry it was cards every Tuesday night with her girl friends from college and an occasional 'girls night out' with the same friends. Usually it was a baby shower, bridal shower, a Tupperware party, an Avon party or something similar, but the constant was the Tuesday night card party. We both had a ritual that we followed when we came home, me from bowling, her from her card party. We both showered before we went to bed and we did it because neither of us smoked, but most of our friends and associates did and neither of us wanted to take the stink of second hand smoke to bed with us for the other to have to smell. At least that was my reason and I'd always thought it was hers too. It was almost midnight when the front door bell rang and I opened the door to find Terry's friend Lea standing there.

"Sorry to bother you, Brad, but Terry had a little too much to drink tonight and I wouldn't let her drive home. I got her this far, but I'm going to need some help getting her out of my car and into the house."

We managed to get Terry out of Lea's car and I carried her into the house and undressed her and that's when I made my discovery.

<<O>>

The clock went off at six and I rolled over and hit the snooze button for Terry and then I got up and headed downstairs. I was at the kitchen table drinking coffee and reading the morning paper when a very bleary eyed Terry shuffled into the room.

"Good morning, party girl," I said and she made a face at me and said, "My head hurts."

I grinned at her. "I shouldn't wonder. When Lea dropped you off last night you were so bombed that I had to carry you into the house and put you to bed."

A worried look crossed her face and I knew what she was thinking, "Did he notice anything? Did I say anything I shouldn't have?" I just smiled at her and behaved as if everything was normal.

"Get some coffee and throw on some clothes. I have just enough time to run you over to get your car before I have to leave for work."

On the ride over to where she'd left the car I said, "So, what did you do last night?"

She looked out the side window. "Nothing. Just shot the shit with the girls and played cards."

I said, "Something must have been different because you don't usually come home so blitzed."

She made a face. "That was Bev's doing. She just came back from Mexico and they had a drink down there they make with tequila and she wanted all of us to try it. That stuff can really sneak up on you."

That isn't all that snuck up on you, I thought, but I didn't say anything.

The following Tuesday I followed Terry to her friend Jana's house where the card party was supposed to be. I parked down the street and settled in to wait and see what might happen. I saw Lea arrive, then Judy and Alice. A few minutes later Joyce and Mary showed up. Nothing out of the ordinary so far and I started to think that I might be wasting my time, but about eight o'clock a car pulled up and three guys got out and went into the house. Ten minutes later a pick up truck pulled up and parked and two more guys got out and went into the house. I noticed that none of them rang the bell. I waited half an hour and then I got out of my car and walked around Jana's house to see what I might be able to see. Unfortunately all the shades were pulled down tight and I couldn't see a thing. I went back to my car and sat and watched the house. At eleven thirty people started leaving and by twelve (and by my count) only Jana, Lea, Terry and three guys were left. At twelve-ten Terry and a guy came out and got in the pick up truck. They sat and talked for about five minutes and then Terry's head disappeared from view and I knew the guy was getting a blow job. I pulled out and headed for home. I wanted to be there when Terry got home. I knew she had just sucked a cock, but I needed to find out if she'd been fucked.

She came in the front door at one o'clock and was surprised to find me waiting for her in the living room.

"What are you still doing up?" she asked.

I gave her a smile and said, "For some reason, sweetheart, I've had you on my mind all evening and thinking those thoughts has me horny as a goat. I've been waiting for you so I can jump your bones."

She gave me a big grin and said, "I'm glad I can still light your fires. Why don't you get into bed and I'll take my shower and then join you."

The grin faded when I said, "No, baby. No shower tonight. I want you here and now" and I dragged her over to the couch and pulled her down. I kissed her and was pretty sure, in fact I was almost positive, that I tasted the salty residue of cum. No surprise there of course, I had just seen her go down on a guy. As I kissed her I ran my hand up her leg and managed to get a finger in her cunt before she could clamp her legs closed. She was wet; she was very wet and I knew if I pulled that finger out and licked it I would taste more salty cum. I wiggled the finger that I had in her and said, "Damn, but you are wet. You must have been thinking of me as much as I've been thinking of you." I saw the expression on her face and I knew she was going to take that idea and run with it.

Sure enough she said, "I've been thinking of you all day, baby. I almost didn't go tonight so we could have stayed home and made love. I'm horny too, but I smell, baby. Let me take a shower."

I grinned and said; "I don't care what you smell like, sweetheart. I want you now just the way you are." I pushed her legs apart and was about to push her panties to one side when she said, "At least let me take my panties off." She lifted her hips as I pulled them down, noticing how wet the crotch band was, and then I put my cock head at the entrance of her cunt. I could read the expression on her face clear as clean glass; "Will he be able to tell?" A little push and I easily slid all the way in. She was as wet and slick as she had been the previous Tuesday and I wondered how many of the guys I'd seen go in Jana's house also went into Terry and I wondered how long it had been going on. In my mind I tried to imagine Terry pulling a train and the thought had the same effect that it had last Tuesday - I couldn't keep my hands off the unfaithful slut. I fucked Terry as hard as I could for a good five minutes and when I came it was so hard I was surprised that I hadn't blown a hole clean through the bitch. I stood up, pulled her off the couch and carried her into the bedroom where I fucked her twice more before rolling over and falling asleep. Next morning over coffee Terry said, "What got into you last night? Whatever it was I hope it keeps on happening." I almost laughed out loud at that one because I had a feeling that it would, at least on Tuesdays.

My discovery that my wife was an unfaithful slut did just the opposite of what I would have expected - it turned me into a sex maniac - I could not keep my hands off the bitch. I especially loved slipping my dick into her when she came home on Tuesdays from her fuckfest. Don't ask me why because I honestly don't have a clue, but there was something deliciously wicked about sliding into that hot sloppy cunt. I don't know if Terry suspected that I might know or not, but she stopped heading for the shower when she got home. Now she would come in and say, "Ready for me, baby? I'm hot and wet for you" and she would strip and we would go at it.

This went on for about six months and then one day I got curious about what it was that got her started and what it was that she actually did on Tuesdays. I took a chance and called Lea and asked her to meet me for lunch. I hoped that she would keep what I was going to ask her a secret from Terry, but if she didn't it wouldn't really matter. Terry was bound to find out someday that I knew what was going on. At the restaurant I cut right to the chase, "I know that Terry is fucking around on me every Tuesday night" and I saw alarm show on Lea's face. "Don't panic," I said, "It doesn't bother me and in fact the knowledge has made our sex life better. I've known now for over six months. In fact I've known since the night you brought her home drunk."

I told her about following Terry that one night and what I had seen. "I don't want her to know that I know because it might change things between us, but curiosity has finally gotten to me and I want to know how it started and what you do every Tuesday besides play cards."

Lea gave me a pensive look; "You really don't care?"

I gave her my 'serious' look and said, "Hell no! In fact I look forward to getting my sloppy seconds every Tuesday."

She looked at me like I was some kind of weirdo and then said, "Too bad my husband isn't like you. Okay, if you really want to know" and she told me the story.

It was a typical Tuesday night card game and around nine o'clock Jana's brother stopped by with three of his friends. They hadn't planned on staying; he had just dropped by to give Jana some tequila he'd brought back from Mexico. While he was there he said he'd like to make them a drink that he'd gotten turned on to while he was there. He made it and they all tried it, and they all liked it. He made another batch, and then another, and another and pretty soon there was a full-blown party going. Terry had gotten blitzed a whole lot quicker than anybody else and pretty soon she was acting pretty loopy and the guys started taking advantage of her. They were kissing her and feeling her up, the girls were laughing and egging her on, and suddenly her tits were exposed and not long after that Todd had his hand up her skirt and a couple of fingers in her pussy.

Todd said, "Does your husband know you behave like this?"

"My husband? Where?"

One of the other guys said, "He's in the other room. He wants to play a game. He doesn't think you can recognize him as fucked up as you are."

Terry said, "I can recognize him" and the guy told her that her husband wanted proof.

"He wants you to be blindfolded and then every guy here will touch your tits or ass and you have to tell from the touch of hands only which one is him."

Somebody handed her another drink, she a big pull on it and was blindfolded. For the next half hour the guys played with her tits, pussy and ass and they kept asking her which one was her husband and all Terry could say was "I'm not sure." Then two of the guys pulled out their cocks and each took one of Terry's hands and put them on their erections. The rest of the guys saw that and they took out theirs and walked over to stand next to the first two. They kept moving Terry's hands from cock to cock and asking, "Is this your husband's?" and Terry kept saying, "I'm not sure. I don't think so, but I'm not sure." And then the inevitable happened and one of the guys said "I guess there's only one way to find out for sure" and he pushed Terry back across the arm of the couch and pushed his dick in her. After that it was orgy time. Of the eight girls there four got up and left, but Terry, Bev, Lea and Jana stayed and spent the next couple of hours being fucked by the four guys (and no, Todd did not fuck Jana). Sometime during the orgy Todd managed to take some video of the proceedings, but no one noticed at the time. The following week Todd and four friends showed up and wanted to play some more, but the girls said no, that the previous Tuesday had been a drunken mistake that wasn't going to happen again. Todd then popped the video in the VCR and said, "How would you girls like hubby to have a copy of this tape?" Every Tuesday since then had been an orgy with Todd showing up with anywhere from three to seven of his buddies.

"To be honest about it," Lea went on, "Terry and I now look forward to Tuesdays and if the tape somehow got lost we would still keep on. I don't know how Terry feels about it, but I'd like to do it on more than just Tuesdays. My husband will be out of town next Thursday. How would you feel about my asking Terry if she wants to come over and play while he's gone?" I was silent for a minute and before I could speak she said, "How would you feel about being a player?"

I was quick to answer that one; "I don't think so. I kind of like things the way they are and I don't want to do anything that might make a major change in our relationship."

"Okay," Lea said. "How about you come over and watch from the closet? If you decide you want to play, come out. If not, Terry will never know you're there."

I thought about that for a bit and then said, "If Terry says she'll do it, I'll try the closet just to see what happens."

Lea smiled and said, "What about now?" I looked at her and said, "What do you mean?" She gave me a smile that could be considered 'smoldering' and said, "All this talk has made me horny. Care to help me out?"

That's another story, but the rest of this one is that the next day Lea called me and said Terry had agreed to next Thursday. All that's left now is to keep a straight face when Terry gives me her excuse for having to go out on Thursday and to get my butt into Lea's closet on time. Life can sure be exciting - if you let it.

The End

-
-
-
-
-
-
-

Vonda's Scoreboard

-
-
-
-
-
-

She was a slut when I married her. All the signs were there; I was just too lost in love (or lust) to have paid any attention. Well, I know now, oh boy do I know now!

I met Vonda at the public library. She was a volunteer worker and donated her time two or three days a week. Sometimes she worked the checkout counter, sometimes she worked in the back cataloging, but usually I saw her stocking the shelves with new or returned books. I was in the library on the average of twice a week and I had noticed her; hell, what wasn't to notice - long hair down to her waist, beautiful face and tits to die for. She was very easy on the eyes and I began to look for her on my visits. I doubt very much that I would have ever spoken to her, but for some disarranged clothing. I was browsing the shelves one-day while she was restocking books. She was bending over putting books on the lower shelf and her top had pulled up exposing part of a tattoo that was on her lower back. "That's not fair," I said to her and she looked around, "Are you speaking to me?"

I said yes and pointed at her back, "Your top rode up when you bent over and I don't think it's fair that I only get to see part of the tattoo."

She laughed and said, "No one gets to see the tattoo unless they are willing to pay the price."

"And that would be?"

"At the bare minimum, dinner and dancing."

"Okay, I'm willing to pay it. When?"

"Tonight works for me. I get off in an hour."

I was using the library's computers to surf the net when she came up to me and told me she was ready to go, "Follow me home so I can drop off my car. On the way you think about where you want to go for dinner, I already know where I want to go dancing."

I liked her 'no nonsense' attitude and thought that she just might be a fun date. When she'd parked her car and got in mine I asked her where we were going dancing:

"It might matter as to what kind of food we eat."

"How are you on country western?"

"Depends. Two-step, shaddish, electric slide and tush-push I can handle, but if it's western swing you want I'm strictly a spectator."

She grinned and said, "I can live with that."

As I pulled out of the parking lot at her apartments I said, "For country western I recommend Mexican, good enough?"

She laughed, "Where have you been, sweetie? I've been looking for you for years."

It was two in the morning when I pulled into the parking lot at her apartments. That was both good and bad. Good because I'd had a great time and the night had flown by, but bad because it was a Tuesday night and I had to go to work in about four and a half-hours. I pulled into a slot in front of her unit, left the car running and got out and went around to open her door for her.

"What are you doing?" she asked. I told her I would walk her to her door and then I had to get going.

"Oh no" she said, "A deal's a deal" and she reached over and took my key from the ignition. "You did the dinner and dancing and now I have to do my part."

She led me into her apartment, told me to have a seat on the couch and told me she would be back in a minute. Two minutes later she walked back into the room naked as the day she was born and as she walked toward me I saw that she had a pierced navel, she had studs through each of her nipples and that she had a ring through a hole pierced through one of her pussy lips.

She also had about five tattoos that I could see and I hadn't even seen the back of her yet. She had a butterfly on the inside of her left breast, a heart just above her pubic area and on the band through the center of the heart, where a name usually goes, it said "All yours."

There was what I can only call scroll work on both of her ankles and on her left arm. She stopped in front of me and turned around and the tattoo on her back was an American eagle. What I had seen in the library was part of the wing spread.

With her back to me she said, "You've seen all my secrets baby except one," and she bent at the waist and pulled her ass cheeks apart. On the inside of the left butt cheek were the words "Promised Land" and a small arrow that could have been pointing either at her pussy or her asshole. She stood up and spun around, "You like?"

I was sitting there speechless and she said, "I was hoping for a better response, baby."

I was an hour late for work that morning and hadn't gotten a minute's rest that night. Vonda was a sex maniac and once she got me going she wouldn't let me stop. She sucked my cock and had me eat her pussy. She had me fuck her and then we went sixty-nine. Next she had me fuck her in her ass and then she washed my cock, sucked me hard again and then we fucked some more. As I staggered out her door at seven in the morning she kissed me goodbye and said, "I'll be home by seven tonight, okay?"

I was at her place every night for the rest of the week and all of the weekend and all we did was fuck. On Monday we went and got our blood tests and on Friday we were married in a civil ceremony. In between Sunday and our wedding we spent every hour that we weren't working together and almost all that time was spent in bed in some form of sexual activity. For our honeymoon we went, where else, to bed and never left it except to eat and go to the bathroom. The last two days before we had to go back to work, we moved Vonda out of her one bedroom apartment and into my two bedroom unit.

My apartment was on the second floor and overlooked the swimming pool and on Vonda's third day there she was sitting on the balcony and I heard her say "Oh my." I went out on the balcony and asked her what was up. She pointed at a guy lying on a blanket, "I think he is."

"He is what?" I asked.

"I think he is up. Look at that lump in his bathing suit. He's cute, I wonder if he's a good fuck?" She giggled. "How about it, baby, want me to find out?"

I said, "Good God, woman, don't you ever get enough?"

She laughed and said, "I thought you already knew the answer to that, baby. No, not ever."

I grabbed her and pulled her into the apartment and fucked her on the floor. When I was done she said, "I guess I'll have to find some more guys that look like good fucks. If this is what happens when I point them out to you I'll have to do it more often."

I rolled her over, "You bitch, you fucking slut you" and I fucked her ass. When it was over she pulled my chain again, "If you're like this when I talk about it I wonder how you'll act when I do it." I reached for her and she rolled away laughing and ran for the bedroom with me close behind. What I hadn't realized at the time is that I was kidding - she wasn't!

I was beat when I went to work on Monday, but somehow I managed to make it through the day. When I got home that night, Vonda, who didn't have to go back to her job until Wednesday, had dinner waiting. I asked her how her day had gone and she said, "It was okay. I just fucked around and then I went and got another tattoo. Want to see?" It was a small star, about half the size of a dime, and it was just under the heart tattoo that said "All Yours."

"What's it mean?" I asked.

She giggled and said, "That's where I'm going to keep score." I must have looked confused (not very surprising because I was) so she said, "You know those old war movies, the ones that show the pilots putting little flags on their planes to keep score of how many of the enemy they shot down?" I nodded a yes and she pointed at the star, "That's my scoreboard."

"What are you keeping score of?"

"Guys I fuck."

Of course I knew she was pulling my chain so I grinned at her. "You little slut, you absolute fucking slut" and I grabbed her and dragged her to the bedroom. Over the next three months we fucked like bunnies and she was always pulling my chain and it always made my dick hard and we always ended up in the bedroom. The number of star tattoos grew until she had over twenty of them. One day she had one with a circle around it and I asked her what that meant and Vonda said, "It means that I let him fuck me in my ass."

I grabbed her and pushed her down on the kitchen floor and fucked her right there as she moaned, "Oh yes, baby, fuck your little slut, fuck me, baby, fuck me."

On weekends she would stand on the balcony and point out a guy and say, "See him? He fucked me Tuesday" or "See that guy over there? This is his star right here" and she would point at one and then laugh as I dragged her into the apartment and into the bedroom.

Another time I said, "I thought you told me that you could never get enough."

"I can't and I don't."

"Yet in over three months you only let yourself get fucked a total of" and I leaned forward and counted the stars "twenty-three times."

Vonda laughed, "That's not twenty-three times, baby, that's twenty-three guys and they have all fucked me more than once. A couple of them fuck me every day," and I hauled her into the bedroom again.

After a strenuous two hours we took a break and Vonda said, "The stars aren't all of it, baby. There are three guys at the tattoo parlor and whichever one puts the new star on gets to fuck me too. He doesn't get a star because that's their pay for doing the job."

"You fucking slut you," I cried as I pushed her down on the bed and fucked her again. You want to know just how dumb I was? One night I asked her, "Isn't it time consuming to have to put all those little stars back on after you shower?"

Vonda laughed, "You wish."

I actually thought that the tattoos were fake ones; the kind you see teenage girls wearing. Not once - not one single time - did I believe that the stars were real and that Vonda was actually doing what she said she was doing to earn them.

Until the night that I came home from work to find Vonda naked except for a pair of high heels. "You're in for a treat tonight, baby. The guy I was going to do this afternoon got hung up and I told him he could come over tonight." Another chain pull, right? I was reaching for Vonda when there was a knock on the door and Vonda said, "Oh good, he's here," and she went over, still naked, to answer the door. She opened it and there was a guy standing there. Vonda took him by the hand and started pulling toward the bedroom, "Catch the door, baby? I'm in a hurry for his cock."

I was standing there staring at them in shock as they disappeared through the doorway into the bedroom. It wasn't until I heard "Ooh, that's a nice one" that I came out of my trance and stumbled over to close the door. By the time I got to the bedroom Vonda had his pants down around his ankles, had him sitting on the bed and was sucking his cock. He glanced over at me nervously and Vonda stopped sucking him long enough to say, "Don't worry about him. He's my husband and it turns him on to know I fuck other guys."

Have you ever been so surprised, so stunned, so caught off guard by something that you were just frozen into immobility? That's what happened to me. I just stood there as Vonda sucked him, fucked him, sucked and fucked him again and then took him in her ass. She was looking right at me and smiling as the guy rooted around in her root cellar and when he came and pulled out of her pooper she told him to go wash his cock in the bathroom and hurry back.

I stepped aside to let him pass and then Vonda came over to me, took my cock out of my pants and started to suck my cock. Then she led me to the bed and said, "Do my ass, baby, while I wait for him to come back" and God help me but I did.

The guy came back into the room and Vonda pulled away from me, "Wash your cock, baby, and come on back. I want to suck you while he fucks me" and I did that too.

I have no idea why I was so docile, but from the time Vonda had answered the door I hadn't said a word, I'd just done what she told me to do. I think I was in some kind of shock. When I came back from washing off my cock Vonda had me lie down so she could suck me off while her lover fucked her from behind. I was lying there with Vonda's mouth bobbing up and down on my dick and I was looking at the face of the guy fucking her and I saw pity in his eyes. His facial expression said clear as day, "You poor spineless sappy bastard" as he pounded his cock into my wife.

When he finally came and pulled out of her she took her mouth off my cock and said "We can save that for later, baby," and she kissed the head of my dick and then got up. She turned to face the guy and said, "Thanks, lover, I needed that," and she went to kiss him, but he turned his face away. He didn't want to kiss Vonda after she'd had my dick in her mouth and he thought I was a wimp. Vonda walked him to the door and then hurried back into the bedroom and started grabbing up her clothes, "Hurry up, baby, get your pants on."

She looked at her watch and said, "If we hurry we got just enough time to make it."

Again I just followed orders with no idea what was going on and as we were going down the stairs to the parking lot she said that since she knew where we were going and we were pressed for time she would drive. Ten minutes later we pulled up in front of a rather dilapidated building with a hand painted sign in the window that said Vinnie's House of Body Art. I watched as Vonda got out of the car and ran into the building and then, like a zombie, I got out of the car and followed her. Just as I got to the door a biker looking type put a hand on my chest and said, "Sorry, pal, we are closing."

I heard Vonda yell, "Let him in, Vinnie, that's my husband."

Vinnie looked me up and down and I saw a smirk on his face as he stepped aside to let me in. Vonda was lying on a cloth-covered table, naked from the waist down, and another biker looking guy was standing next to her with a tray of things. "Have a seat, baby" and then to the guy standing there, "Another star, Billy, and put a circle around it."

The tattoo didn't take all that long; what took the time was Billy and Vinnie fucking her. First Vinnie fucked her while she sucked Billy's cock and when Vinnie came they switched. By the time Billy came she had Vinnie's cock hard again and that time he fucked her in the ass. He came and Billy took his place up Vonda's butt while Vinnie came over to me.

"Glad to see how it's done, pal? Come back any time, we don't charge for lessons."

That was the wrong thing for Vinnie to say. I'd had enough! The pity in the first guy's eyes, the look that said I was spineless, Vinnie's smirk when I came in the door and now the taunting. Whatever fog that I had been in suddenly lifted.

Vinnie had a goatee and my hand shot up and grabbed it and I jerked his head down onto my knee. My knee caught him right under the chin and Vinnie went down like a bag of rocks. I stood up and kicked him in the ribs as hard as I could and as he lay on the floor looking groggily up at me I said, "You got any more smart mouth shit you want to lay on me, asshole?"

By then Vonda had pulled away from Billy, leaving him there with his cock waving in the breeze, and had run over to us. "Baby, have you lost your mind? Help him up, go ahead, give him a hand."

I shrugged and reached a hand down and he took it and I helped him up. He looked at me, rubbed his jaw and said, "Sorry, man, I didn't understand."

He didn't understand? And he thought I did?

Vonda said, "Now you two shake hands. I won't have there being any animosity between you two. Vinnie, you had no reason to talk to him like that and baby, what got into to you? Honestly, if I didn't know better I'd think you were jealous or upset."

Vinnie and I shook hands and Vonda said, "Come on, baby, you and I have some unfinished business to take care of at home." As we were walking out the door she turned and said, "Sorry, Billy, I'll make it up to you next time."

On the way home Vonda said, "You had no reason to do that to Vinnie."

I wanted to scream "I had every god damned reason in the world! I just found out my wife is fucking anything that moves, is keeping score on her body and I'm supposed to remain calm?" But I didn't say that. What I said was, "Doesn't it bother you that other men think I'm a spineless wimp. That I sit or stand around and watch them fuck you because I'm not man enough to do it myself? That asshole as much as said it to my face and I'm supposed to just sit there and take it?"

"Oh don't be silly. They know you are man enough for me. Vinnie and Billy have known me long enough to know that I would never have married a man who couldn't handle me. You have no call to get upset when other guys look at you and think you're a wimp just because I'm out getting strange cock. You know better! You know I love you and that you own me heart and soul."

She was quiet for a few moments and then said, "Maybe I should work you in on some threesomes and foursomes - give you a little more confidence in yourself. Think you could handle a gangbang? Maybe seven or eight guys? We could do it at our place this Friday. No, for your first one I think we should hold it at five guys, five guys and you. Yes, I think that would be best; six is a nice round number, I can do three of you while the other three rest and catch their breath. Should we have refreshments? How about just beer and pretzels, or maybe chips. No dip though, people are always spilling it and I don't want to have to clean the carpet when they leave. Did I tell you I'm thinking of getting a stud through my tongue? I saw a nice one the other day and it even had matching earrings and a navel ring. Do you think it would be better in silver or gold? Say, I know what you can get me for Christmas. How about a belly button stud with a diamond in it. Wouldn't that be cool?"

I just sat there and shook my head in absolute wonder and amazement and listened as she drove us home.

~~The End~~

*Watch out for *Erotica Short Stories, Vol. 8 - Wild Urges*

Becoming a Shared Wife, Vol. 4 –

(Fulfilling Her Needs)

Becoming a Shared Wife, Vol. 5 –

(Rachel)

Becoming a Shared Wife, Vol. 6 –

(Sharing My Wife)

Becoming a Shared Wife, Vol. 7 –

(Sarah)

Becoming a Shared Wife, Vol. 8 –

(Cuckolds & Shared Wives)

Becoming a Shared Wife, Vol. 9 –

(Her Forbidden Fantasy)

A Just Plain Bob Christmas

Barbara Jean

Filthy Steps in the Office

My Perfect Wife: And Her Dirty Little Steps

Annabelle Gets Caught

All Filled Up!

Patio with a View

Boyfriend's Corrupted Steps

Never Never

His Wife's Doppelganger

Just A Back-up Guy

Secret Revenge

A Weird One

Becoming a Shared Husband, Vol. 1 –

(Suck Me)

Becoming a Shared Husband, Vol. 2 –

(Husbands Who Stray)

Becoming a Shared Husband, Vol. 3 –

(Get even!)

Becoming a Shared Couple, Vol. 1 –

(Steamy Swingers)

Erotica Short Stories, Vol. 1

(Taboo Desires)

Erotica Short Stories, Vol. 2

(Nasty Steps)

Erotica Short Stories, Vol. 3

(Married But…)

Erotica Short Stories, Vol. 4

(Sizzling 10)

Erotica Short Stories, Vol. 5

(In My Wife's Panties)

Erotica Short Stories, Vol. 6

(Taboo Unlimited Desires)

From the Author

If you enjoyed any of my books then please share the love and promote my books in Amazon.

If you write me a review and send me an email I will send you a free book, or many.
(Just know that these emails are filtered by my publisher.)

Good news is always welcome.

One Last Thing, For Kindle Readers...

When you turn the page, Kindle will give you the opportunity to rate this book and share your thoughts on Facebook and Twitter. If you enjoyed my writings, would you please take a few seconds to let your friends know about it? Because... when they enjoy they will be grateful to you and so will I.

Thank You!

An Open Letter from Just Plain Bob

A message for those who like my stories, those who hate my stories, those who are indifferent and those who have yet to make up their minds.

I have often stated that I really don't care what others think about my stories, that I write for my own enjoyment and then I offer to share. If you like my stories fine and if you don't, also fine since I have already satisfied my target audience - me!

It is human nature to strive to get better. If you take up bowling your first games are going low scoring, but you will work and practice to get better and as your average climbs you may forget the game where you had three gutter balls and shot an eighty-six, but that game is still there in your past.

Your first time on the golf course you shot an eighty on the front nine, but did you settle for that being your game or did you work to improve? You may eventually get a three handicap, but that nine hole eighty is still there as part of your past.

When you hired in at your job did you say, "Cool, I got it made" and do nothing more than what you barely had to do or did you go to work thinking that, "Someday I'm going to be running this place." You might never climb that high, but human nature says that you are going to at least try.

It is the same with authors who write stories and post them on sites like Literotica. Their first stories might not be all that good, but comments and feedback along with a desire to get better drive them toward putting out a better product or to at least try.

I'm no different. My first stories might not have been all that great, but they are still there on the hard drive. I like cheating wife stories and five years ago I found my first adult site that catered to cheating wife stories. It was a pay site, but it had a policy of giving a free lifetime membership to anyone who submitted five stories to the site. How hard can that be I said to myself as I sat down and fired up the word processor and went to work.

I sent my five stories in and sat back to enjoy my free membership and a funny thing happened. I started getting feedback, most of it positive, and I became hooked. I started cranking out more stories. The site I was sending my stories to had seven categories:

Bisexual
Cream Pie

Groups
I Watch
Gang Bang
Racial
SM/BD

I know nothing about bisexual or SM/BD and I had no interest in Groups so all the stories I wrote I tailored for the four remaining categories:

Cream Pie
I Watch
Gang Bang
Racial.

I turned out eight stories a month, two for each category, which means that after five years I have over 120 stories in each of those categories and they are all still on the hard drive.

A year ago I received an email asking me why I never posted stories on Literotica. The answer? I didn't know about Lit. I pulled it up, liked what I saw, and started sending in stories to it. All new stories? No, not hardly, not with over 400 stories sitting on the hard drive. Maybe one new story for each fifteen or so old ones. The newer ones are better, at least I think they are and I have received some feedback that leads me to believe that others think so too, and I will continue to write new ones.

But I am still going to recycle what is on the hard drive, stories that were written specifically to fit the four categories. That means that those of you who hate cream pie stories still have eighty or so to look forward to. Ditto for those who call me a racist; you will get another seventy or so interracial stories.

Those who hate wimps will only see about fifty more of those because the stories I sent to the I Watch category were split 50/50 between what some call wimps and some call "real men." Why the 50/50 split? It came from listening to the readers. I would get feedback asking me why all the men in my stories were hard asses. "In real life men are more forgiving, especially if it is the first indiscretion." So I would write stories with forgiving husbands and boyfriends and then the next batch of feedback would say, "Why are all your husbands spineless wimps" and I'd write stories that went back the other way.

Eventually I came to realize that I was wasting my time - there was no way I could write a story that would satisfy everybody and that is when I adopted my philosophy of writing for my own enjoyment and then offering to share.

As far as the gangbang stories? Well, what can I say? Gangbangs are gangbangs and there are still eighty or so of them to go.

The bottom line is that Literotica readers are going to see more of my old stories than my new ones. If I'm still around three or four years from now it will probably go the other way, more new than old.

I feel the need to respond to some of the comments and emails I have received. By far the largest percentage comes from people who say, "You are an asshole because all women are not whores and sluts and that's all you make them out to be."

Next most common is, "You must really hate women you sick fuck."

"You must be a wimp because all the men in your stories are wimps" is up there in the top ten along with, "Why don't you give it a rest and go crawl off in a hole somewhere."

There is a lot more, but I'm only going to address those four and in reverse order.

I won't stop and go crawl in a hole because I am enjoying the hell out of what I am doing and remember what I said, I am doing this for MY OWN ENJOYMENT and then I offer to share. Some obviously like my sharing with them and so I will continue to do so. No one is holding a gun to a reader's head and telling them they must click on a Just Plain Bob story or die. It is a conscious choice on the reader's part to move that mouse and click on that story.

When a man finds out he has a cheating wife or girlfriend there are only a limited number of ways he can handle it. If he loves her he can forgive, try to forget and try to hold on and somehow make things work. He can turn his back on her, walk away and get on with his life. The third option is to take revenge.

According to a good portion of those who send me feedback the first and second options are proof that the men are wimps. If the man takes the third option he is still considered a wimp if he doesn't do some sort of physical damage to the woman and her lover. These readers believe that the only way not to be a wimp is to kill, maim and destroy everything in sight. Doing that however, will invariably get the man throw in jail and that is why it so rarely happens in real life.

In real life most revenge takes place in the man's head when he says to himself, "I should have _____ (fill in the blank) the fucking cunt!" I know this because I have been there and done that (see The Dark Trilogy). In my stories I try to mirror real life so kill, maim and destroy are going to be for the most part absent. Outside of some fisticuffs there will be very little physical violence in my stories. Most of my husbands are going to do what I did, what several of my friends and others that I know have done, forgive, or walk away. If this makes them wimps and me a wimp for writing the story that way, so be it.

Next is the "I must hate all women." Nothing could be farther from the truth. I love women. I lust after women. I even like whores and sluts. I have been married four times, engaged two other times (that did not end in marriage) and I have always had girlfriends between marriages. My philosophy is that women were put on this earth for me to enjoy and I'm not talking just sexually. I could sit at the mall (and have) for hours and just girl watch.

The engagements, girlfriends and three of the four marriages bring me to the #1 anti JPB comment on the list.

"You are an asshole because all women aren't whores and sluts."

Well dear reader, you can not prove that by me! I will say up front that I KNOW all women aren't whores and sluts, BUT the majority of the women in my life were. My mother ran around on my father for years while he was driving a truck for a living. My Aunt Margaret cheated regularly on my Uncle Bill, as did my Aunt Mildred on my Uncle Paul. My Aunt Betty fucked around on my Uncle Bob for years and finally left him for his brother, my Uncle Wendell. Uncle Wendell in turn caught her on her knees at his company Christmas party giving Season's Greetings to his boss.

My sister is three times divorced and each divorce came about when the then current husband caught her out spreading pollen. Both of the engagements I mentioned ended when I found out that I was not the one and only and a lot of the girls I dated between marriages never made it to engagement status for the same reason.

And that brings me to my three ex-wives. The first one, Helen (I believe I commented on her in the intro to The Dark Trilogy) had seven different lovers before I found out what was going on. I was living proof that love is blind. Ditto with my second wife. She had a secret life that she hid from me and when I found out about her brother, his friends and the gangbangs she was history.

My third marriage ended in divorce because of a different kind of cheating (and I can just imagine the outrage I am going to get over this) - she cheated on me with an idea. I was away from home on business, she was lonely, a couple of Jehovah's Witnesses knocked on the door and my wife, with nothing better to do invited them in. When I came home from my trip I found out that she had found God. On a scale that runs from TRUE BELIEVER on one end to ATHEIST on the other you will find me just to the right of AGNOSTIC and since I would not allow myself to be SAVED the marriage eventually died.

So yes, I write about sluts and whores because as everyone knows, you tend to write about the things you know. And I do like sluts and whores, just not the ones that lie to me and cheat on me.

So be forewarned - if you click on a Just Plain Bob story you will be getting sluts, whores and husbands who do not kill, maim and destroy. There are other things you will rarely find in a Just Plain Bob story. Even though I try to mirror real life my stories all take place in StoryLand. In StoryLand STDs and unwanted pregnancies do not exist unless the author feels like they may add something to the story. Bad things do not happen in StoryLand unless the author so wills it and no amount of "You should have..." in comments and feedback will change a story already posted.

Lastly, I will touch on a truth. None of what I have written here means shit because the same readers will still read the same stories that they profess to hate and make the same comments they have always made. Knowing this, I will deliberately post stories that will have them frothing at the mouth.

It is the least I can do for an adoring public.

Thank you!

Just Plain Bob
justplainbob@awesomeauthors.org